For Phil – J.B.

PUFFIN BOOKS

UK | USA | Canada | Ireland | Australia | India | New Zealand | South Africa

Puffin Books is part of the Penguin Random House group of companies
whose addresses can be found at global.penguinrandomhouse.com.

Penguin
Random House
UK

First published 2009
This edition published 2013, reissued 2021

001

Text and Illustrations copyright © John Butler, 2009

The moral right of the author and illustrator has been asserted

Printed in China

The authorized representative in the EEA is Penguin Random House
Ireland, Morrison Chambers, 32 Nassau Street, Dublin D02 YH68

A CIP catalogue record for this book is available from the British Library

ISBN: 978–0–723–28668–4

All correspondence to: Puffin Books, Penguin Random House Children's
One Embassy Gardens, 8 Viaduct Gardens, London SW11 7BW

FSC
www.fsc.org
MIX
Paper from
responsible sources
FSC® C018179

It was Bedtime in the Jungle

John Butler

PUFFIN

It was **sunset**
in the jungle,

And the **sky** was
streaked with **red**.

The **animals**
were **calling**,

It was nearly
time for bed . . .

It was **bedtime**
in the jungle,

And the **day** was
almost **done**.

A **rhino** lay
down close

to her baby
one.

"Sleep," said her mother.

"I'll sleep," said the one.

And they slept in the jungle, as the day was almost done.

It was **bedtime**
in the jungle,

And the **stream** was
shining **blue**.

A **monkey**
made a **bed**

For her babies
two.

2

"Rest," said their mother.

"We'll rest," said the two.

And they rested in their bed, by the **stream shining blue.**

It was **bedtime**
in the **jungle**,

And **beneath** a
leafy **tree**

A **leopard**
tucked her **paws**

Round her babies
three.

"Snuggle," said their mother.

"We'll snuggle," said the three.

And they snuggled up together, beneath the leafy tree.

It was **bedtime**
in the jungle,

And the **sun**
shone no more.

A **Wolf**
nuzzled noses

With her babies
four.

4

"Nestle," said their mother.

"We'll nestle," said the four.

And they all began to nestle, as the sun shone no more.

It was **bedtime**
in the jungle,

And the **moon**
would soon arrive.

A **tiger**
gently licked

All her babies
five.

5

"Quiet," said their mother.

"We'll be quiet," said the five.

And they quietly closed their eyes,
as the moon would soon arrive.

It was **bedtime**
in the jungle,

And in a **nest**
of sticks

A **peahen** smoothed
the feathers

of her babies
six.

"Hush," said their mother.

"We'll hush," said the six.

And they hushed side by side, in their nest made of sticks.

It was **bedtime**
in the jungle,

And the **stars shone**
in heaven.

A **wild pig**
snuffled softly

Round her babies
seven.

"Settle," said their mother.

"We'll settle," said the seven.

And they all settled down, as the stars shone in heaven.

It was **bedtime**
in the jungle,

And the **hour** was
getting **late**.

A **duck**
gave a kiss

to her babies
eight.

8

"Cuddle," said their mother.

"We'll cuddle," said the eight.

And they cuddled up close, as the hour was getting late.

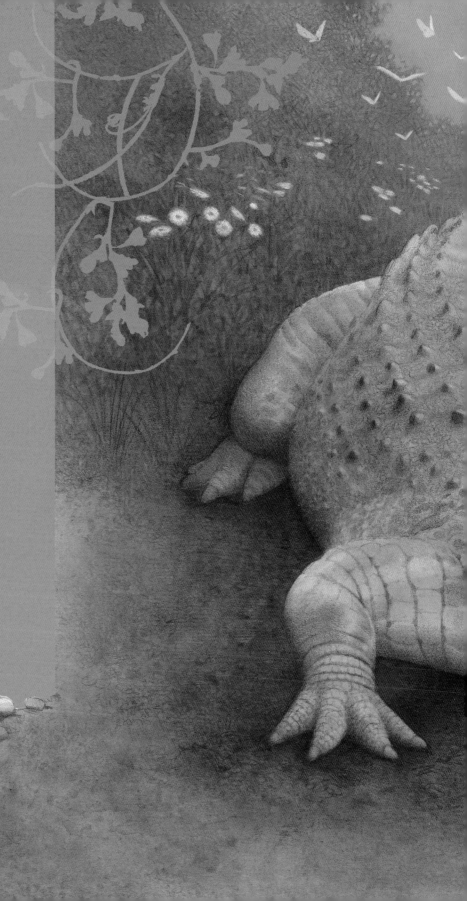

It was bedtime
in the jungle,

And the **moon**
began to **shine**.

A **crocodile**
was lazing

With her babies
nine.

"Snooze," said their mother.

"We'll snooze," said the nine.

And they all snoozed together, as the moon began to shine.

It was bedtime
in the jungle,

And by the
river bend

Elephants were
gathering

all their babies
ten.

10

"Dream," said their mothers.

"We'll dream," said the ten.

And they dreamt beneath the stars

It was night-time
in the jungle,

And the moon shone
full and bright.

All the
jungle babies

were safely
sleeping tight.